Perfectly POPPY

Outside Surprise

Story by Michele Jakubowski

Pictures by Erica-Jane Waters

Curious

First published in the UK by Curious Fox,
an imprint of Capstone Global Library Limited,
7 Pilgrim Street, London, EC4V 6LB
Registered company number: 6695582

www.curious-fox.com

Illustrations by Erica-Jane Waters

ISBN 978 1 782 02201 5
19 18 17 16 15
10 9 8 7 6 5 4 3 2 1

A CIP catalogue for this book is available from the British Library.

Table of Contents

Chapter 1

Millie's New House

On Saturday, Millie called
Poppy with some fun news. Millie
was Poppy's best friend.

"My dad is building me a
playhouse in the back garden!"
Millie said.

"That is so cool. What kind of

playhouse is it?" Poppy asked.

"It's like a tree house," Millie

said, "but it will be on the ground.

He's been building it all day."

Poppy tried to imagine the playhouse. It would probably have big chairs, a TV, and a lot of toys. Maybe they could even have a sleepover in it!

Poppy didn't love playing outside. But this playhouse sounded pretty cool. In fact, it sounded perfect!

"I'll be right over," Poppy said.

Chapter 2

The Little House

When Poppy got to Millie's

house, she raced to the back

garden. She found Millie standing

in front of a small blue house.

Millie looked really excited.

Poppy was surprised. This was
not what she thought the playhouse
would look like.

Instead of a door, a sheet hung
in the doorway. It had windows, too,
but there was no glass in them.

"Isn't it awesome?" Millie asked.

Poppy didn't know why Millie was so excited. It wasn't anything fancy at all.

"Um, yeah," Poppy said. She walked into the playhouse.

It was empty. Where were the toys and games and TV? Where were the big chairs?

"What should we play first?" Millie asked.

Poppy thought and thought.

Finally she asked, "Well, what do

you do in a playhouse?"

"That's the best part," Millie said. "We can play whatever we want to play! We just need to use our imagination!"

Chapter 3

Poppy's Place

Millie and Poppy got some snacks to help them think of what to play. They were inside the playhouse munching on some crackers and cheese when they heard a noise.

Poppy poked her head out of
the front window. She saw her
older brother Nick and his friend
Thomas.

"This is so cool!" Nick said.

Just then Poppy got an idea.

"It is cool. In fact, it's a really

cool restaurant called Poppy's

Place," she said.

Millie poked her head out of a
window on the side.

"You place your order here," she said. "Then you go round to the other window to pick it up."

Nick and Thomas raced over to Millie's window.

"Welcome to Poppy's Place!

Today's special is a burger, fries,

and a milkshake," Millie said.

"I'll take one," Nick said.

Millie and Poppy pretended to
be cooking the food. Poppy was
having so much fun!

Then Poppy stuck her head
out the window and handed Nick
some pretend food.

"Here you go, sir," she said
with a big smile.

The four of them took turns

being the customers and working

in the restaurant.

After that they brought out

some of Millie's stuffed animals

and played pet shop.

Nick, Poppy, Millie, and Thomas
agreed that they would play something
different every day.

"We can play pirates!" Nick said.

"We can bring out our dolls and play house," Millie said.

"We can even play school," Thomas said.

"That's the best thing about this playhouse," Poppy said. "With our imagination, we can play whatever we want!"

Poppy's Diary

Dear Diary,

Today I went to Millie's house to see her new playhouse. At first I didn't think it was anything special, but now I see how lucky she is! I wonder if my dad will build one for me?

Sometimes it's hard to think of what to do. But with our imaginations, we can play anything! Playing outside turned out to be a lot of fun. But when it rains, I like to stay inside!

Poppy

Build Your Own Playhouse

You don't need a lot of supplies to make your own playhouse. It can be as simple or as fancy as you want. Grab boxes, pillows, blankets, sheets, or anything else that might work. Be creative!

The Card Table Cottage

Have an adult set up a card table (or other small table) for you. Grab a sheet or blanket and cover the table. If you have an old sheet, you might be able to cut out windows or draw on it. Be sure to ask permission first.

The Pillow Palace

Grab as many pillows and blankets as you can. Stack up the pillows and drape the blanket over the top. (Hint: Use couches or chairs to help keep the blankets up.) You might want to get a torch, as it might be a little dark in your pillow palace.

The Cardboard Castle

Look around your house for extra boxes. They can be big, little, or medium. If you find a big enough box (from a large appliance), you could make your entire playhouse out of that. If you find lots of boxes, build up walls as high as you can. Be sure to grab felt-tips and decorate your cardboard castle!

Perfectly POPPY

The Big Bike £3.99
9781782022008

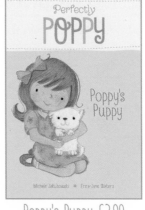

Poppy's Puppy £3.99
9781782021988

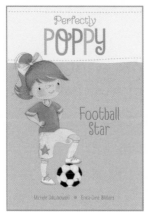

Football Star £3.99
9781782021995

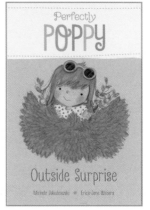

Outside Surprise £3.99
9781782022015

Read all of Poppy's adventures!
Available from all good booksellers.